# Chapter One

The sun was rising on Booty Bay.
On board the *Barracuda*, seven fierce-
looking pirates were getting ready to
set sail.

Captain Cutlass was leaning against the wheel, trying to read his compass.

"Glasses!" squawked the parrot on his shoulder.

"Hold yer beak, Peggle!" said Captain Cutlass.

Peggle grabbed her beak with her claw.

Captain Cutlass put on his turtle-shell glasses and checked the compass. Peggle removed her claw. "Glasses, glasses, glasses," she squawked softly, nibbling the captain's gold earring.

"Shhhhh!" said the captain. "It's our little secret, remember! If the crew find out I need to wear glasses, they'll make me walk the plank!"

A huge pirate with an enormous, red beard stomped up.

"What were you saying about glasses, cap'n?" asked Fearsome Fergus politely, scratching his beard with his hook.

Captain Cutlass quickly put his glasses in to his pocket. He buttoned his jacket over his tubby tummy, grabbed his cutlass and turned around. "I said, 'pirates don't wear glasses!'"

"Aye, aye, cap'n!" said Fearsome Fergus, and he went off to tell the others.
Peggle sighed and fluffed up her feathers.

The sun rose over the *Barracuda*'s bow. Captain Cutlass put on his pirate hat and called the crew together. He held up a tattered map in one hand and his cutlass in the other. "This is a map of Treasure Island!" he said. "And we're off to find it!"

"Aye, aye, cap'n!" roared the pirates, who were struggling to keep the sun out of their eyes.

Salty Sally put on her sunglasses.
"Take them off!" said Fearsome Fergus.
"If the captain sees, he'll make you walk
the plank! He says pirates don't wear
glasses!"

Salty Sally trembled, and her pigtail
drooped. She quickly took off her
sunglasses. "Sorry," she said. "But I
don't think he saw me."

She was right. Captain Cutlass was pointing towards the rising sun with his cutlass. "Raise the anchor, me hearties!" he said. "Treasure Island's that-a-way!"

# Chapter Two

In the middle of the day, in the middle of the ocean, a huge albatross flew across the sky.

It cast its shadow over the *Barracuda*. "Where did that cloud come from?" said Captain Cutlass.

# SPLAT!

"Boggle me eyeballs! It's smelly, white rain!" he said.

"Glasses!" squawked the parrot.
"Hold yer beak, Peggle!" said Captain Cutlass. "Pirates don't wear glasses!"
Peggle sighed and rolled her eyes.

The *Barracuda* was white and sticky.
Captain Cutlass turned to his crew.
"Swab the decks, yer scurvy scallywags!"
he roared.
"Aye, aye, cap'n!" said the pirates.
Then they set to work in the hot,
bright sun.

Salty Sally put on her sunglasses.
"Take them off!" said Fearsome Fergus.
"If the captain sees, he'll make you walk
the plank! He says pirates don't wear
glasses."
"Sorry, I forgot!" said Salty Sally.
"But I don't think he saw me."

The pirates were busy scrubbing the decks. No one noticed the tentacles slithering up the side of the ship. A giant squid was trying to sink the *Barracuda*!

"This seaweed gets everywhere," said
the captain, as he walked along the deck.
He prodded a mass of waving tentacles
with his cutlass.

"Glasses!" squawked the parrot.
"Hold yer beak, Peggle!" said Captain
Cutlass. "Pirates don't wear glasses!"
Peggle sighed and covered her eyes
with a wing.

The *Barracuda* was covered with slimy
tentacles.

"Clear the decks, yer lily-livered
layabouts!" roared Captain Cutlass.
"Aye, aye, cap'n!" said the pirates.
Then they began to wrestle with the
giant squid.

"There's no stopping us now, Peggle,"
said Captain Cutlass. "Treasure Island
here we come!"
Peggle peeped out from under her wing.
She watched the pirates struggling with
the tentacles. Then she sighed and
covered her eyes again.

# Chapter Three

Late that afternoon, the pirates were pulling off the last of the tentacles when WHUMP! the *Barracuda* ran into an enormous whale.

"Boggle me eyeballs!" said Captain Cutlass. "Another pirate ship! It must be the *Jolly Jonah* trying to get to Treasure Island, too."

"Glasses!" squawked the parrot. "Hold yer beak, Peggle!" said Captain Cutlass. "Pirates don't wear glasses!" Peggle sighed and shrugged her feathers.

The pirates were staring at the whale.
"Board that ship, yer motley mongrels!"
roared Captain Cutlass.
No one moved.
"Don't just stand there!
Follow me!"

The captain grabbed hold of a
rope tied to the mast and
swung across to the
whale. Peggle clung
tightly on to his
shoulder.

SLAP! The whale's tail sent Captain
Cutlass and Peggle spinning through
the air.

They landed in the crow's-nest as
the whale sank beneath the waves.
Peggle settled back on the captain's
shoulder and fluffed up her feathers.
"Glasses!" she squawked.

There was no one in the crow's-nest, so the captain put on his glasses and looked around.

"Glasses, glasses, glasses!" Peggle squawked softly, nibbling the captain's gold earring.

"Shhh!" said Captain Cutlass. He put his glasses in to his pocket and called down to the crew. "We sank the *Jolly Jonah*!" The pirates looked at each other. "And I can see Treasure Island!" the captain went on. "It's over there!" "Arrrrrrr! Treasure Island!" cheered the pirates.

Captain Cutlass climbed
down the rigging with
Peggle on his shoulder.
"Stow the sails, me
hearties!" he roared.
"Land ahoy!"
"Aye, aye, cap'n!"
said the pirates.

# Chapter Four

SWOOOSH! CRUNCH! THUNK!
The *Barracuda* ran aground on
Treasure Island.

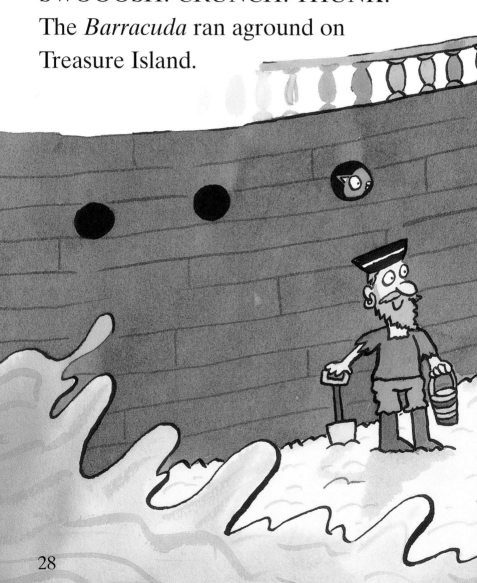

The pirates climbed down on to the sand.

Captain Cutlass took out the treasure map and tried to read it.

"Glasses!" squawked the parrot.
"Hold yer beak, Peggle," said Captain Cutlass. "Do I have to keep telling you? Pirates don't wear glasses. If the crew find out, they'll make me walk the plank!"

He turned to his crew. "Dig here!"
he ordered, pointing to a spot with his
cutlass. "No, here! No, I mean here!"

Peggle sighed and stuck her head under
her wing.

The setting sun sparkled on the sea.
Salty Sally put on her sunglasses.
"Take them off!" said Fearsome Fergus.
"Do I have to keep telling you? If the
captain sees, he'll make you walk the
plank! He says pirates don't wear glasses!"

"OK..." said Salty Sally. "But I don't
think the captain sees anything much,
do you?"

Three days later, there were more holes in Treasure Island than in a Swiss cheese, and the pirates still hadn't found any treasure.

The crew of the *Barracuda* were sweaty,
frazzled and dazzled.
The pirates had all had enough.

Salty Sally was sulking. Fearsome
Fergus's face was as red as his beard.

"You're a crummy, clueless captain!" barked Fearsome Fergus. "You can't tell an albatross from a cloud. You can't tell a giant squid's tentacles from seaweed. You can't tell a whale from a pirate ship. You can't even read a treasure map! If you don't think of something quick, we're going to make you and your moth-eaten parrot walk the plank!"

"Arrrrrrrr! The plank!" roared
the pirates.

Captain Cutlass and Peggle looked at one another and gulped.

"Glasses!" they squawked together.

"Eye, eye, cap'n!" roared the pirates. And as the captain put on his glasses, Salty Sally, Fearsome Fergus and all the pirates put on their sunglasses, too.

"Boggle me eyeballs!" said Captain Cutlass. "Pirates *do* wear glasses!"

# Chapter Five

Captain Cutlass looked carefully at the
treasure map. "Well, I never!" he said.
"I've been holding it upside down all
this time!"

He turned the map the right way up.
"Glasses, glasses, glasses," squawked
the parrot.

"Aye, Peggle," said Captain Cutlass. "It's easy to see when you're wearing glasses. This is where X marks the spot. Right here, under my feet!" Then he put down the map and his cutlass, and picked up a spade.

Peggle perched in a palm tree, and the pirates sat in the sunshine and sang sea shanties. They watched Captain Cutlass get sweatier and sweatier as he dug deeper and deeper... and deeper... until...

CLUNK! His spade hit something.
Captain Cutlass wiped the sand off his
glasses. "I can see a chest!" he yelled.
"A treasure chest! Come and help me,
yer lazy lumps!"

"Aye, aye, cap'n!" roared the pirates.
Then they leapt to their feet.

The sun was setting as the sweaty pirates heaved and pulled the treasure chest out of the hole.

Peggle flew to Captain Cutlass's shoulder. "You've been very quiet since I put on my glasses," said Captain Cutlass.

Peggle blinked. She watched as the pirates gathered round.

Then Captain Cutlass threw open the
lid of the treasure chest.

"Arrrrrrrr! Treasure!" cheered the
pirates. "Hooray for Captain Cutlass,
the pirate who wears glasses!"

"Well, Peggle," said the captain. "What do you say to that?"

Peggle stared at the pile of glittering gems and gold. Then she looked at the smelly pirates. She fluffed up her feathers and wrinkled her beak…

"Bath time!" squawked the parrot.
The pirates roared with laughter.
"Hold yer beak, Peggle!" said Captain
Cutlass. "Pirates don't take baths!"